SUMMARY

OF
MIDNIGHT SUN

by

Stephanie Meyer

OMNI READS

Note to Readers:

This is an unofficial summary & analysis of Stephanie Meyer, Midnight Sun, designed to enrich your reading experience.

Scan here to buy the original book.

Disclaimer: All Rights Reserved. No part of this publication may be reproduced or retransmitted, electronic or mechanical, without the written permission of the publisher, with the exception of brief quotes used in connection in reviews written for inclusion in a magazine or newspaper.

This book is licensed for your personal enjoyment only. This book may not be re-sold or given away to other people. If you would like to share this book with another person, please purchase an additional copy for each recipient. If you're reading this book and did not purchase it, or it was not purchased for your use only, then please purchase your copy.

Product names, logos, brands, and other trademarks featured or referred to within this publication are the property of their respective trademark

Our Free Gift to You

We understand that you didn't have to buy our Summary book.
As a token of our appreciation, we are happy to give you a free gift.

Scan this QR code to get it before it expires!

Table of Contents

Summary of *Midnight Sun*

*M*idnight Sun is set in 2005, mostly in Forks, Washington, USA. It is told through the point of view of Edward Cullen, who is a 108-year-old vampire living there with his family of vampires, the Cullens. The Cullens are unique not only because they don't hunt humans for their blood, as most of their kind does, but also because they don't opt for a nomadic life as is the norm. Instead, they choose to pose as and mingle with humans, and only move from place to place every few decades to avoid suspicion and being revealed for who they are because they don't age. They also choose areas that are very cloudy most of the year, like Forks, so that they can go out during the day. Unlike the classic vampire myth about the sun being deadly to them, the real issue is that the sun makes their skin reflect and refract the light in an unnatural way. Being in the sun would, therefore, reveals their nonhuman nature.

To be able to stay in a location for as many years as possible, most of the younger-looking Cullens pretend to be high schoolers when they first arrive.

Going through high school feels like purgatory for Edward, who is consistently bored there. Edward can read minds, which is an ability that is unique even among vampires. To him, everyone's mind broadcasts thoughts, which is like a constant hubbub surrounding him and which he has to tune out. The lessons in high school have nothing to offer him since he holds at least two medical degrees and keeps collecting college diplomas as he repeats the process of education over time.

The other vampires posing as his siblings are in different grades, namely Alice, Rosalie, Jasper, and Emmett. As a result, they have other issues that they grapple with when being in high school. Jasper especially faces a constant challenge controlling his hunger for blood and hunting humans, something Edward feels he has mastered. Generally, the Cullens consider Edward an extremely disciplined vampire with immense self-control that is not tempted by the humans surrounding him or their delicious blood fragrance.

This situation changes drastically when, suddenly, a new student arrives by the name of Isabella Swan. She happens to be in his Biology class. At first, Edward snorts at the excitement that runs through the entire school at the new student arriving, thinking it infantile and a typical shallow reaction of human teenagers. He believes that the new arrival does not concern him, yet he is still mildly annoyed since it makes everyone's thoughts louder and somewhat more obnoxious.

Edward listens to the thoughts of the teenagers regarding Bella. He does it to make sure that nothing is being discussed that could, in any way, put his family in danger of being revealed. That's how he already knows that Isabella prefers being called Bella and that she is the daughter of the chief of Forks' police. Otherwise, he finds her uninteresting and unimpressive.

However, this drastically changes when Isabella walks into the Biology classroom. Her scent hits Edward fully. It overwhelms him and makes him desperately hunger for her. The sense, and the draw of her blood, is very intense. It makes him entirely become the predator that he is. Edward can barely hold back his urges to attack her. He even fantasizes about killing all the students in the classroom to eliminate witnesses. Edward spends the entire period thinking about how to kill her and struggling with himself. As soon as the bell rings, he runs. He takes refuge in his car to escape Bella and her smell.

There is another disconcerting thing about Bella; Edward can't read her mind. Her thoughts are a mystery to him, as much as everyone else's is a loud broadcast. He doesn't know what to make of that. Compounded with the problem of her scent, which brings up the monster in him, Edward starts feeling hatred towards Bella.

The first solution he tries to give to this problem is to change classes. However, Edward soon realizes that there is no way he can change courses and graduate. Though he successfully charms the secretary into making every effort to satisfy his request, Edward still is thwarted. A chance meeting with Bella, who had also gone to the secretary's office, convinces Edward that he has to avoid her at all costs. Her scent is making him mad and very dangerous for every human around him.

He resorts to escaping Forks for a while, running to Denali, Alaska. Edward has a deep connection to Carlisle, the vampire who is a father to him. Carlisle is a very benevolent person. He abstains from killing humans and cares for them as a doctor. Edward looks up to him and wishes to make him proud, as Carlisle values human life and protects it.

Edward died in his late teens in 1918 of the Spanish Flu. Carlisle was the one that turned him into a vampire and helped him in the first years of his adjustment.

However, when Edward still was a very young vampire, he had been influenced by other vampires, and he left Carlisle to hunt humans and experience drinking their blood. Initially, he enjoyed this different, more vampiric lifestyle. This was because he only hunted humans that had, in some way, lost their humanity and became predators themselves, such as murderers and rapists. Soon, however, it began to weigh him down and to make him feel wrong about the monster Edward was becoming despite his vigilante-style hunting. So, he returned to Carlisle and stayed with him, abstaining from human blood ever since.

During his brief stay in Denali, he meets with a friendly vampire, Tanya. Tanya is attracted to Edward, but he isn't interested. Still, she is friendly enough to talk with him and help him settle his thoughts. After talking with Tanya, he decides to return to Forks and his family who are missing him. He chooses to face Bella's temptation head-on.

Going back to high school now is like walking a tightrope for Edward. He has to be constantly vigilant and continuously keep his urges under an iron grip. He regulates his breathing, doing it minimally and only to be able to talk, especially in Biology class. He pays extra attention to all the thoughts of the people that are around or are thinking of Bella since he can't read hers. His inability to read her mind makes him deeply curious about her. He begins watching her for more than just his struggle with bloodlust for her.

He quickly starts being concerned for her as he watches her. His sincere concern for Bella develops because he gradually begins to piece together her personality and character. It stands out to him as intelligent and selfless. She always puts the needs of others before her own, something that is endearing to Edward. Though initially, she looked plain to him, now he begins finding her attractive and unconventionally beautiful.

In parallel, he also pays more attention to the personalities of the students that surround Bella and who accost her more frequently. He dislikes Jessica Stanley, who is disingenuous. Her friendly behavior towards Bella is incongruent with her jealous and mean spirited thoughts about her. This dissonance grows as Jessica realizes how Edward Cullen, who is considered school royalty due to his gorgeous looks and off-standish behavior, pays more attention to Bella than anyone else.

He also dislikes Mike Newton, and his lewd thoughts about Bella, as he tries to become her boyfriend, though unsuccessfully. On the contrary, he likes Angela Weber as he enjoys the positive environment of her mind when he reads her thoughts to watch Bella.

In his efforts to overcome his weakness to Bella, Edward starts overtly befriending her in Biology class. In their interactions, Bella is astute enough to catch Edward when he slips in his façade as a human. Her intelligent questioning increases Edward's interest in her but also his alarm. He fears she is potentially becoming dangerous for the integrity and safety of his family.

Bella generally doesn't react in ways Edward expects. Because he can't read her thoughts, the interpretation of her behavior becomes a fascinating puzzle for him.

Things become a lot more complicated, though, when Edward saves Bella from a deadly car accident. He steps between her and a careening van that was skidding on ice in the school parking lot. Not only does he stop the van, but he puts a dent in another car as he shields Bella twice from getting crushed. In the process, Bella hits her head. Edward tries to use that to lie to her when she calls him out on his superhuman speed and strength.

This event brings upheavals and clashes among Edward's vampire family as well. Rosalie especially is upset because she doesn't want to uproot and move to a different place, where she will need to go through high school again. But his brothers Emmett and Jasper voice concerns as well. On the other hand, Alice, who has the gift of seeing the future, is worried about Edward and his psychological state. Carlisle is proud of Edward for saving Bella and for being so self-controlled despite her smell. His wife, Esme, is only worried about the harmony within the family.

Bella has agreed to cover for Edward, on the agreement that he will explain his supernatural strength and speed. However, instead of keeping his promise, Edward stops talking to her and denies that what Bella remembers was real. He treats her with hostility to get her to distance herself from him and his family.

Still, he worries about her, and he watches her through other people's minds. He also fights with and opposes his siblings Rosalie and Jasper. They want to kill Bella to make sure that their secret is not revealed. But killing Bella is a plan that Carlisle also disapproves of. When Alice gets a vision that Bella is going to be her friend, killing her is forever abandoned as a plan.

But Edward is now thrown into a different kind of turmoil because Alice sees two futures for him and Bella. One in which he kills her and drinks her blood, and one in which she also becomes a vampire. Edward is terrified that he will end up killing her. He is also directly opposed to turning her into a vampire because he thinks of vampirism as a curse.

Edward sees himself as a monster and his existence as not a life. He doesn't want that for Bella. He wants her to grow up, go to college, get married, and have children as every normal human does. Despite Alice's conviction that he can't change the future, he is determined to do it.

When a dance comes up where the girls are supposed to ask the boys, not the other way round, Edward finds he is jealous of every boy that Bella might invite. He is delighted when she refuses to ask anyone. She tells them all that she will be going to Seattle during the weekend of the dance.

Edward decides to talk to her again then. She talks back to him angrily, convinced that he had been hostile to her because he regretted saving her from the van. The notion infuriates Edward, but he doesn't try to explain things to Bella. He is overcome by a fear that, because she is clumsy and very accident-prone, anything might happen to her while he isn't there to protect her. At the same time, he wants to be as far away from her as possible, so that the futures that Alice saw won't happen.

Edward is pushed by this fear of unreasonable dangers that might happen to Bella, including imagining a meteorite crashing through her room. As a result, he climbs into her bedroom while she's sleeping. He sits in her bedroom, watching her sleep, and contemplates leaving for good. He listens to her talk in her sleep when suddenly, she calls out his name. In her sleep, she repeats his name and begs him not to go.

He decides to stay. He feels that he can now control his bloodlust for Bella to the point that he doesn't quite feel it. He also decides never to turn her into a vampire. Instead, he is determined to create a different future, where he will live with Bella, keeping her human, for as long as she wants him.

He openly befriends her again every day at school, and they start getting along. Edward becomes happier, and he starts composing music again, to the delight of his vampire parents. Rosalie becomes more resentful while Jasper and Emmett are confused or amused, depending on the occurrence. Bella is accident prone after all, and Edward takes it upon himself to protect her from all kinds of hazards.

Watching Bella makes him elusive to his family as he follows Bella around even when he's not with her at school, and she doesn't see him there. He's happy that when he, along with his family, is absent from school due to it being a very sunny day, Bella is unhappy and clearly misses him.

When Bella decides to go shopping with her friends, Jessica and Angela, in Port Angeles, Edward follows from afar, intent on protecting her from any harm. By now, he is convinced that she attracts trouble like a magnet. However, because it is quite sunny, he has to wait in the shadows, and he often loses sight of the girls.

When he manages to get near, he realizes that Bella has left the girls for a while. Mad with worry, he tries to look for her by scanning through the thoughts and minds of strangers. When Edward finally sees Bella through the mind of a man, he realizes this man, Lanny, is a dangerous criminal. He listens to his gleeful thoughts on how he intends to attack and eventually murder her.

Edward is enraged. He hurries, homing in on the man and his flunkies who are crowding around Bella to prevent her from fleeing. Edward realizes that the others are drunk while Lanny is quite sober and malicious. He decides to exact terrible revenge on him, but after he saves Bella.

He drives through the dark street where the ambush against Bella is taking place, effectively cutting the men's access to her. Bella gets in the car, and they drive off. Edward is more concerned with Bella's wellbeing, so he returns her to her friends. However, they have just finished eating, whereas Bella has had nothing to eat. So, Edward treats her to dinner.

On the drive back, Bella reveals to Edward that she has been to La Push. In La Push, old friends of her father had warned her of the Cullens. She tells him that it doesn't matter to her what Edward is. That's when Edward confesses to her that he is a vampire. She is inquisitive, and for the first time, he answers her questions about his nature directly.

Later, he consults with Carlisle regarding the men who tried to assault Bella. Edward doesn't want to become a killer again, since Bella openly cares for Edward, even for a terrible criminal. However, he also doesn't want to let Lanny loose on the streets. Carlisle is proud of Edward for his restraint, and assures Edward he'll see to the matter personally, which Carlisle does. The criminal, Lanny, gets arrested for several murders he had committed previously.

Edward and Bella are now seen openly as a couple at school, which scandalizes a lot of students. Rosalie, too, is incensed and throws several fits. Alice is thrilled and is waiting for her opportunity to talk to Bella and start on becoming friends. Edward still doesn't quite let her. He develops a game of sorts with Bella: they ask questions about each other, taking turns every day.

A complication happens though when Billy Black, a member of the Quileutes and hostile towards the Cullens, sees Edward with Bella at Bella's house. The Quileutes and the Cullens are upholding an old treaty of mutual peace, but there is due suspicion and dislike on the part of the Blacks. However, nothing happens to destroy Edward's and Bella's plans. Alice meets Bella for the first time, but they don't talk much.

Later, she warns Edward that the day he has planned with Bella is crucial and extremely dangerous for their future. He is running the risk of losing control and hunting her. If that happens, he will kill her. Nevertheless, Alice gives him hope. If he manages to get through the day without killing or turning Bella into a vampire, there is a new future where they can be a couple. A couple where Bella remains human.

The weekend of the dance arrives. Bella still is not going to attend. She will pretend to go to Seattle, but in reality, she plans to be with Edward for the entire day. She wants to see why he avoids the sun if the sun does not kill vampires.

Edward is very nervous about this, though he dresses accordingly. When he finally shows himself to Bella in the sun, in the middle of a beautiful meadow in the woods, she loves what she sees: Edward sparkling like marble and diamonds under the sun.

That is the moment where the crisis happens. Edward is suddenly is too close to Bella's jugular as she tries to hug him, and he almost bites her. He rushes away from her, but gradually he gets back into control. To his amazement, Bella has not left, nor has she begun to fear him.

They sit in the meadow, and finally, Edward tells her everything about himself and his family without hedging or avoiding answering her questions. With each answer he gives Bella, Edward fears she will become disgusted or fearful of him and abandon him. But she never does. They kiss for the first time, and he only feels joy, not bloodlust.

He tells Bella of how Carlisle became a vampire in the 1600s, and how later he turned Edward, then Rosalie, then Emmett on different occasions of extreme need and desperation. He talks about how Alice and Jasper joined their family. He mentions how Alice doesn't know who created her or the circumstances of her turning.

Bella listens to all of it attentively, and she never once flinches away from Edward or his family. Even when he confesses that he has been entering her bedroom every night to watch over her, she's only worried about having embarrassed herself with her words while sleeping. Edward's countenance becomes a lot more optimistic. He now has hope for his future with Bella. She wants him to stay in her bedroom. When she eventually sleeps, she says, "Edward, I love you," in her sleep.

Later, Rosalie is enraged. When Edward asks her to be kind or at least polite to Bella, she reveals the reason why she can't: she envies Bella for still having her human nature. Rosalie misses being human, and she resents Bella for being ready to give it up. Edward assures Rosalie that he does not intend to turn her into a vampire. Rosalie is doubtful he will manage it. She considers Edward's plea, but when she realizes that Bella will be meeting the Cullens by next day, she just leaves.

Meeting Edward's family is somewhat stressful for Bella because she's anxious for them to like her. They love her because she makes Edward very happy. They still give Bella wide berth, to get used to them. Edward shows her around the house and tells her of Carlisle's story, with Carlisle's permission. She learns not only how Carlisle became a vampire, and his story after that, but also about Edward's time away from him when he was hunting humans.

That day, Alice predicts there is going to be a storm, and Emmett wants to play baseball. The Cullens invite Bella to watch the game, and she immediately accepts. Edward takes Bella home so that she can eat before that. That's where she encounters Billy Black, who is looking to talk to her father. Bella makes sure to tell the man she's aware of what the Cullens are, and that he is not to interfere with her choice to be with them. Billy is stunned by Bella's intensity, and he backs off without telling Charlie anything.

Meanwhile, Edward leaves to inform his family about the Blacks, but also to coax Rosalie into playing the game. He suggests to her that it might be a start in tolerating Bella. Rosalie reluctantly agrees.

Edward picks up Bella from her house and meets Charlie officially as her boyfriend for the first time. Then he takes Bella to the remote area in the mountains where the Cullens will play baseball, which they simply call 'the clearing.'

The way the vampires play baseball is intense because they use all their speed and all their strength to do it. The sheer noise they make is why the need to mask their game with the thunderstorm. Bella is very impressed and enjoys watching the game, even though she usually doesn't like sports.

However, the game is cut short because Alice is hit with the vision of three strangers approaching them. They are newcomer vampires named Laurent, James, and Victoria, who seem only interested in taking part in the baseball game. Carlisle is confident they are in no danger, even with Bella there, because they are seven against the three strangers. But they agree that it would be a mistake to have Edward flee with Bella because then they would be able to hunt Edward down with her and outnumber him.

Jasper uses his unique gift, as the strangers' approach, to keep their attention away from Bella and away from himself as a potential adversary. Carlisle is polite and welcoming, and the new vampires seem to be friendly.

Carlisle almost manages to get them to follow him back to the house, away from the clearing.

However, the weather changes and the wind sends Bella's smell directly in the path of the new vampires. Their instincts kick in, especially James', and he tries to attack Bella. Edward cuts him off, and James is surprised. This obstruction creates a challenge for him, especially when the Cullens openly state that Bella is off-limits, and part of their group.

When Laurent states that they won't harm Bella, James turns on him. Victoria sides with James. Though on the surface nothing happens, Edward knows that James will not give up.

Bella has become James' new goal: to snatch her from the Cullens and eat her. Edward realizes that his unique gift is to be a tracker. He won't be dissuaded from getting her, nor will he give up. Alice says there's only one way for him to give up: for Bella to stop being human and become a vampire.

Edward will not hear it. He is determined to preserve Bella's life and deal with the tracker vampire differently. The Cullens, together with Bella, devise another plan, to throw off James' tracking and keep Bella safe. Edward, Carlisle, and Emmett will try to throw James off Bella's trail, while Rosalie and Esme protect Charlie. Bella, with Alice and Jasper, will drive to Phoenix and lie low until it's safe for Edward to get her and leave for the actual hiding place of his choice.

Edward hates having to separate from her, but he concedes. He takes Bella back to her father, where she pretends to have an emotional reaction to being tied down to Forks and a man, even Edward. This eruption rings similar to what made Bella's mother break up with Charlie, so he believes her.

Laurent apologizes for James. He gives them due warning that James is a very potent vampire with high intelligence and determination to kill both Edward and Bella. Edward is determined to hunt James, with Carlisle and Emmett, as soon as Bella is away and safe. Despite Rosalie's resentment and reluctance to help Bella in any way, Esme and Rosalie go guard Charlie's place.

Initially, it looks like James takes the bait and tracks Edward's rather than Bella's team. However, it turns out that James anticipated the ambush that the Cullens tried to spring on him, and instead, he leads them in a wild goose chase all the way to Vancouver. From there, he takes a plane and successfully escapes without Edward or Carlisle having any idea where he is headed.

Alice finally manages to see in a vision that James is headed to Phoenix and is targeting Renee, Bella's mother. She warns Edward that James is going to spread the Cullens too thin, thus making them easier to face in combat. Edward, Emmett, and Carlisle decide to take a commercial flight to Phoenix to arrive there as quickly as possible. Alice, Jasper, and Bella are supposed to meet them at the airport's terminal.

However, things don't go as planned. Bella gets a call from her mother, and before Alice can realize it, she vanishes. She leaves behind a note of apology: James has lured her away from the Cullens by threatening her with her mother's life.

It is now almost hopeless to find her before James kills her. However, Alice does have a vision of where she will be with James. They steal the fastest cars they can find, to get there in time before Bella bleeds out.

It is agony for Edward because, through Alice, he can see Bella being hurt by James. They manage to sneak up on the place where he is keeping her without James noticing. Edward bursts in the room and yanks James off Bella's prone body. He throws him to Jasper and Emmett, who kill him.

Edward and Carlisle give Bella first aid until they realize that James has bitten her, and his venom is going to change her into a vampire. They are now faced with the option of hurrying along with her change into a vampire or killing her. Alice presents Edward with a third option: to suck the venom out of her body before it can change her.

Edward decides to try, even though it's perilous since he can lose control and kill her. Still, he manages to suck out the venom and stop himself before he goes on to drink her blood, even though he loves the taste of her.

Once her condition is as safe as possible, the Cullens have to deal with the matter of transporting her to the hospital. They must set things up, so her injuries look like the result of an accident. Alice takes that up, and she masterfully sees into the future to pick the best scenario. She makes it look like Bella tripped over a flight of stairs in a hotel and crashed into a window. Because she is accident-prone as a rule, everyone in her family believes this.

Edward is overcome with guilt about what happened to Bella. He blames himself and contemplates leaving her. But Alice has warned him that if Edward does this, Bella will be profoundly depressed and will remain emotionally crippled and unhappy. When Bella wakes up, she confirms this, telling Edward he has to stay with her.

Meanwhile, Alice gives Edward a camera with a video of James's attack on Bella. He had been recording it all so that he could emotionally torture Edward with it. In it, Edward sees how courageous Bella is, but he also hears James talk about something unexpected: Alice's origin. The vampire who changed Alice did it to save her from becoming James' food, in the 1920s. James lost interest in Alice, but he killed the vampire in revenge.

Edward decides to stay with her until she grows out of her love for him. When they return to Forks, the students believe the story of Bella's accident. They also consider her and Edward a serious couple. Charlie is nervous about the abrupt seriousness of this relationship between Bella and Edward, but Carlisle puts his mind at ease.

Finally, Edward takes Bella to the prom. Alice gives Bella a makeover in a beautiful dress, and Edward dresses formally in a tux. Bella is disappointed that the occasion is the prom and not a ceremony for changing her into a vampire. She also isn't thrilled about going to the dance where she's likely to be very clumsy and unable to dance. Her leg is still in a cast. Edward takes her to the prom and dances with her despite the cast. She asks him to change her into a vampire, but he refuses. He promises to stay with Bella for as long as she wants him. They both profess their love for each other, and the story ends at that point.

The Setting of the Story

*M*idnight Sun is set in 2005, in the United States of America. Most of the story takes place in the very cloudy, dimly lit town of Forks in Washington. However, we also get some good glimpses of the snowy peaks of Denali, in Alaska, as well as the blindingly sunny Phoenix, Arizona.

There are also glimpses in history that we get when the past of the vampire characters is explored. For example, we take a look at Chicago in the 1930s and London in the 1640s. Strong, albeit brief, comparisons of society in those eras with society as it currently is are drawn. Predicaments of previous times sometimes catch up with the main characters, or past traumatic events are subtly shown to be non-issues in today's world.

For the main character, Edward, and his family, money is no problem. However, it would not be correct to claim that the Cullens are part of the upper class. Instead, the family of vampires stands outside the social structure of the human world. This classlessness holds true for the other vampires we encounter in the story, be they nomads, vagrants, or hermits of some sort.

Bella Swan is decidedly middle class, as are the students portrayed in Forks' high school where the main characters attend. What affluence there is always has a limit, and the resources available to them are finite.

The weather is also an essential element in the story: Forks is almost always cloudy, wet, and moody. Phoenix, on the other hand, is brightly sunny and hot. The expectations are subverted in that it's the cloudy, broody town that offers protection in the story. In contrast, the sunny city is where the most significant threat exists: not only for the vampires but also for the human. The same goes for the wind, which carries Bella's scent: it is enough to undo any plan and immediately turn a relatively harmless situation into a highly threatening one.

Story Plot Analysis

In essence, *Midnight Sun* is the story of a couple falling in love and facing adversity that stems from their different nature.

Edward is a vampire. He is an apex predator designed to hunt humans. Everything about him seems to be built for this purpose. Humans find him irresistibly attractive, as he has superhuman strength, speed, and sense of smell, and he is indestructible.

Bella is a mortal human with blood that attracts vampires. She becomes irresistible to Edward, but as prey, not as a person.

Initially, any relationship between them seems impossible. Their nature makes it impossible for them to interact or connect on a level field.

And yet, this is precisely what happens: love bridges the chasm that separates them.

As the story is told from Edward's point of view, we vividly live through every high and low in the emotional roller coaster that his attraction to Bella brings.

It isn't Bella that brings Edward's struggle with his nature as a predator. This is something that he has been struggling with for decades in his century-long life. The challenge that Bella forces him to deal with is conquering his nature, not merely handling it.

When Bella comes into Edward's life, he believes that he has reached a plateau in his development. He thinks that he has already mastered his unique life choices. Despite that, there is dissonance in his heart because Edward's self-esteem is, in reality, very low despite his superficial haughtiness. Because he is a vampire, he is convinced that he is a monster, a villain, the thing that heroes kill in stories.

Edward's vampire family, the Cullens, deal with this by abstaining from hunting humans. They limit themselves only to killing animals for their blood. However, this choice is a torturous one, as their nature urges them to drink human blood instead. The scent of humans can, at times, be irresistible.

When the scent of a human is alluring enough, a vampire's instincts can completely take over his/her thoughts. If that happens, then the vampire is nothing more than a killing machine, unable to restrain him or herself. Going against this urge is physically painful and emotionally straining. And yet, the Cullens manage to fight this urge. In this way, they stand on two boats: that of being human and that of being the monster.

Edward believes he is the best, after his father Carlisle, in doing that. He prides himself on being superior to humans and in control of his monstrous nature. When Bella arrives at the school with her sweet, irresistible blood scent, all of Edward's well-practiced control crumbles.

He comes very close to killing her several times and even considers murdering other people to get to her. This realization that the monster in him is still strong and roaring shatters his self-image. Bella becomes a symbol of what he must overcome, the challenge he thought he'd dealt with, and now rises before him with seemingly insurmountable odds.

Bella is also the only individual, vampire, or human, whose thoughts he cannot read. It makes him unable to interpret her behavior as well as that of other people. This forces him to pay attention to her as an individual, while at the same time, he struggles with the relentless urge to drink her blood.

The constant struggle makes him fall in love with Bella, as he gets to know her better, further complicating his predicament.

It is only when he uses his mind, and the love he has for her, as a weapon to beat down the monstrous side of him that he ultimately succeeds. Edward is rewarded with the chance to have human emotions and experiences he never thought would be open to a vampire.

The vampire tracker in the end that seeks to destroy Bella serves as Edward's ultimate test: not only a test of his love for a mortal woman but also a test for the conquering of his nature.

Experiencing the story through Edward's view, we feel that the entire goal is for him to reach the level at which Bella already is. She has transcended her fear of him, overcoming her nature, and her love for him is absolute and unconditional. Her devotion baffles Edward since he has never seen it in a mortal. In truth, Bella's purity of heart and emotions serve as the example he seeks to follow, whether he realizes that or not.

Main and Secondary Character List

Main Characters

Edward Cullen: A 108-year-old vampire who looks 17 and pretends to be a high schooler. He can read peoples' minds—all except Bella's.

Isabella (Bella) Swan: A mortal girl in the same class as Edward. She has just arrived at Forks to live with her father and is the new arrival at Forks' high school.

Secondary Characters

Alice Cullen: A young-looking vampire and Edward's sister. She can see visions of the future but doesn't know who created her and who she was before she became a vampire.

Jasper Cullen: A young-looking vampire and Edward's brother. He can manipulate people's emotional state.

Emmett Cullen: A young-looking vampire and Edward's brother. He has extraordinary strength, even for a vampire.

Rosalie Cullen: A young-looking vampire and Edward's sister. She has extraordinary beauty.

Carlisle Cullen: A vampire from the 1600s who is the father and leader of the Cullen family. He is a doctor for humans and has inspired all of the vampires in his family not to hunt humans. He created Edward, Esme, Rosalie, and Emmett.

Esme Cullen: A vampire and Carlisle's wife. She is the mother for all the other vampires.

Jessica Stanley: A mortal high schooler and one of Bella's closest friends.

Angela Weber: A mortal high schooler befriending Bella.

Mike Newton: A mortal high schooler who tries to woo Bella.

Charlie Swan: The chief of Forks' police and Bella's father.

Renée Dwyer: Bella's mother.

Tyler Crawley: A mortal high schooler who almost kills Bella with his car, and later tries to woo her.

Billy Black: A Quileute Native American living in La Push, who dislikes the Cullens and knows their secret.

Jacob Black: Billy Black's son, who is developing a crush on Bella.

James: A tracker vampire who loves the challenge of the hunt.

Laurent: A vampire that passes through Forks together with James and Victoria.

Victoria: James' partner vampire.

Brett Warner: A registered nurse at the hospital where Carlisle works.

Tanya: A vampire that lives in Denali and who is friendly with the Cullens.

Irina and Kate: Vampires that live with Tanya in Denali.

Tara Galvaz: A struggling classmate in Edward's and Bella's Biology class.

Peter and Charlotte: Vampires that are friendly towards the Cullens.

Ben Cheney: A classmate of Edward's and the object of affection of Angela Weber.

Mr. Banner: Edward's Biology teacher.

Ms. Cope: The secretary in Edward's high school.

Maria: The vampire that created Jasper in the late 19th century.

Lanny: A dangerous criminal that is passing through Port Angeles.

Siobhan: A female vampire that lured Edward into hunting humans when he was still a young vampire.

Maggie and Liam: Members of Siobhan's coven.

The Volturi: The de facto vampire police force, who make sure all vampires abide by specific rules.

Dr. Sadarangani: A doctor in Phoenix. He is a friend and colleague of Carlisle's.

Gloria: Bella's RN in the hospital in Phoenix.

Chapter 1: First Sight

We are introduced to Edward and his thoughts. It's through his eyes and his emotions that we follow the entire story.

Edward considers high school a kind of limbo. He calls it purgatory and considers himself above the mortal teenagers that attend it with him. Because Edward can read minds, vampire and mortal ones alike, he can watch things that take place through other people. When everyone's mind is overcome with excitement at the arrival of the new student, a girl named Bella Swan, Edward remains unimpressed. He looks down on this general wave of excitement, which he considers infantile.

He focuses more on his siblings, other vampires that have become part of the Cullen family over the ages. Through his eyes, we are introduced to the vain but breathtakingly beautiful Rosalie, the still-somewhat-feral Jasper who struggles with the scent of human blood, and Alice, who sees visions of the future and can warn the rest of imminent threats of any kind.

We are also introduced to a few mortal students: Jessica Stanley, who used to have a crush on Edward, and Mike Newton, a popular boy among his peers. Edward thinks little of them, mainly because he reads their thoughts and finds them shallow or unsavory.

What draws his attention about the new girl, Bella, is that he can't read her thoughts at all. Seeing that Jessica has accosted her as a new best friend, while thinking pretty nasty thoughts about Bella, makes Edward feel oddly protective towards her. The reaction, together with the fact that he can't read her thoughts, makes him feel uneasy. He is determined not to let this anomaly about the girl's thoughts make him obsess about her.

However, when Bella comes to sit beside him in the Biology classroom, he is hit with her scent. Her scent, to him, is unlike any other human's. It's the most alluring, the most delicious, and the most irresistible. It immediately turns him into a predator. The urge to attack and drain her of that delicious blood is so overwhelming he even considers killing the entire class to do it.

It's only the thoughts of his father, Carlisle, who believes in him to be better than the vampiric predatory nature, and his resistance to murder, that saves Bella and the class that day. But, every minute in it is agony for Edward.

As soon as the bell rings, Edward flees and hides in his car for a while, before going to Ms. Cope's office to try and change his Biology class so that he won't be with Bella. However, this proves to be impossible, even though Ms. Cope is charmed enough by Edward to want to help him.

While he is there, he crosses paths with Bella again. Once more, he is overwhelmed by the urge to kill her for her blood. The urge is so strong that he flees the school and the town.

Are you enjoying the book so far?

If so, please help us reach more readers by taking 30 seconds to write just a few words on Amazon.

Or, you can choose to leave one later...

Chapter 2: Open Book

Edward has taken refuge at Denali, in Alaska. There, another vampire named Tanya meets him. She initially thinks he's there for her, as she had propositioned Edward before. However, even when Edward tells her that he's not there to accept a proposal of mating or casual relations, she stays to talk with him. She professes her reassurance that Edward will conquer the challenge that Bella has presented him.

He returns to school, determined to rise above the challenge, and make his parents, and especially Carlisle, proud. He is somewhat surprised that Bella hasn't talked about their uncanny encounters with anyone. He watches her through the minds of Jessica and Mike, and tries to puzzle her out, since he can't read her thoughts.

This curiosity is further enhanced when, as he tries to chat Bella up, Edward makes a mistake in calling her Bella rather than Isabella. Bella catches it and calls him out on it, which is something he didn't expect. The same happens almost immediately after when she asks him about the color of his eyes. It makes Edward pay a lot more attention to her and even begins thinking of her as attractive in an unconventional way.

Through their conversation, Edward realizes that Bella is a very selfless person with low self-esteem. The selflessness attracts him, and the irony that Bella considers herself an open book because her face is expressive is not lost on him.

However, his fascination with her frightens him. He doesn't want to be attracted to her or interested in her because that raises the risk of him killing her, of giving in to the allure of her blood. And yet, even when he tries to avoid her, he thinks about her and finds her cute and amusing.

Chapter 3: Risk

Carlisle is fully supportive of Edward's choices, even though he doesn't understand why he stays in Forks when Bella creates such a risk for him. Edward isn't sure why either, and he decides that he will leave after one last day at school. He realizes with dismay that Bella, her feelings, her personality, and her actions, fill his world in a way nobody has before. His attraction to someone, that awakens the monster within him so intensely, is something that scares him and solidifies his decision to leave.

The next day, as he is in the parking lot thinking of how to set up his story about leaving, an accident happens: Tyler Crawley loses control of his van, which heads straight for Bella. Edward knows that if he allows the accident to develop without interference, Bella will die.

So, he steps in to grab her out of the way of the van. Then, he has to save her again, as the vehicle skids towards her, by stopping it with his hand. Bella witnesses both his superhuman strength and his superhuman speed. When Edward tries to suggest that she imagined it all, or that it was a false memory from hitting her head, she refuses to believe it. She insists that she saw him being superhuman. Edward desperately asks her to cover for him and accept his version of events for others. She agrees on the condition that he explains the situation later. Edward agrees.

Later, however, when Bella is proclaimed to be alright, Edward refuses to give her an explanation. He tries to make her dislike him by being aggressive and cold to her, gaslighting her in the process. He hates having to do this, but he keeps to it.

Chapter 4: Visions

Edward's actions have caused a great upheaval among the members of the Cullen family. The fact that Bella witnessed Edward's powers is too significant of a threat of exposure for the vampires. A few of Edward's siblings, namely Rosalie, Jasper, and Emmett, are willing to kill Bella to keep their secret from being revealed. Edward is determined not to let them.

In the end, it proves that he won't have to. Carlisle is definite that every life is precious, including human beings. He doesn't want them to kill Bella, even if the risk of exposure is there. Edward assures them all that Bella doesn't intend to talk about what she has seen. The younger vampires are not convinced until Alice tells them that, indeed, Bella will not give away their secret. She adds that she is going to be close friends with Bella.

This shocks Edward. He quickly becomes the target for teasing by his brothers, since Alice reveals that he will be in love with Bella if he isn't already. Rosalie is disgusted by this development, and envious. Distressed, he declares that he will leave Forks, but Alice tells him this is impossible. Carlisle, as well, is against it because if Edward leaves, it's more likely that Bella will talk about them.

When Alice tells him that there are only two futures for Bella, one where she becomes a vampire and one where she is killed, he rebels. He is determined to make a third future for her.

Chapter 5: Invitations

Edward carries on through school, but it is torturous to him. He keeps listening to the students' thoughts to detect whether Bella talks about him. But she never says anything except the cover story that she'd agreed to repeat.

During Biology, he cuts off communication with her, and Bella doesn't try to initiate it again. He resorts to watching her through the eyes and minds of others. In this way, Edward gets to know of her more, watching her behavior and parsing out her intent behind it. He sees even more how considerate she is of others, and how much she strives to help them in indirect ways. Edward progressively becomes engrossed in her, although he forbids Alice from going near her to befriend her, as Alice has foreseen.

He is also becoming jealous of the boys that try to get her attention. This makes him feel embarrassed, considering he'd looked down on such things before.

The spring dance is coming up, and Edward watches how boys try to get Bella to invite them to the event since custom has it that the girls are the ones who will ask the boys. The jealousy burning him, he talks to Bella again for the first time since the hospital. Edward is shocked then, to realize that Bella believes he regrets having saved her life. It makes him angry, but he doesn't explain anything to her.

Instead, he watches her reject every boy that comes up to her regarding the dance. He takes pleasure in seeing the rejections and gets hope that she might be interested in him despite his behavior.

Together with this hope comes the fear that all kinds of accidents might hurt Bella. He is convinced that she is accident-prone and a magnet for trouble. He is so worried that he sneaks into her bedroom at night to watch her sleep. He knows his behavior isn't right, but he can't help himself.

Watching her sleep, Edward realizes he loves Bella. He believes that the best thing for Bella would be for him to go, so that she can have a normal, fulfilling mortal life. He hears her talk in her sleep, asking him not to go. Edward is torn because he doesn't want Alice's vision of Bella as a vampire to come true.

Still, he patches things up with her and offers to give her a ride to Seattle, where she said she would be going on the day of the dance. He warns Bella that it's not prudent to have him as her friend, but that he wants to be her friend anyway. Bella accepts his invitation, and he is delighted that out of all the boys who gave her invitations, Bella said yes to him.

Chapter 6: Blood Type

During lunch hour, Edward invites Bella to sit with him at a table. He warns her again that he isn't a good friend for her, but that he is done trying to stay away. Through the tentative dialogue, they begin to get to know each other directly. Bella tells him she's trying to figure out what he is. However, when he coaxes a theory out of her, Edward realizes she doesn't have a clue. It relieves him, and it gives him teasing fodder. He does give her a hint though that he's dangerous. Bella refuses to believe that he is bad, despite Edward suggesting it.

Edward skips Biology because they will be doing blood typing, and he doesn't want to risk being near Bella while her blood is exposed. He waits in his car when he sees Mike trying to help Bella to the infirmary. Bella has fainted. Edward rushes to take her himself, to Mike's dismay.

Edward helps her skip Gym class, and learns that she has plans to go with friends to La Push over the weekend. He's jealous that Mike will be there. But Edward gives her a ride home and uses it as practice for the car ride to Seattle. He ruminates about the loving couples in his family: Carlisle and Esme, Rosalie and Emmett. He feels that his love for Bella doesn't match any of the romances he's witnessed.

Chapter 7: Melody

Sitting in his car, Edward breathes in Bella's smell and ruminates about their relationship. He wants Bella to be attracted to him but knows she shouldn't be. His love for her, along with the bloodlust, is making him very conflicted. But because he has seen definite signs that Bella likes him, he feels inspired.

He starts playing the piano and composing again, to Esme's great delight. He realizes that Rosalie is jealous of Bella. Rosalie is scandalized that Edward would be attracted to a mere human rather than a beautiful vampire like herself, even if she is not interested in Edward at all. She is mortified that Edward reads this in her thoughts.

When he learns that two friendly vampires will be arriving soon, Edward decides to stay close to Bella to make sure no accidents happen. Though they don't hunt in the Cullens' territory, Edward can't trust them not to lose control over Bella's blood's allure.

When Bella is back from the beach excursion, Edward gets in her bedroom to watch her sleep again. He is a bit worried that she went to La Push: that's where the Quileutes are, and they know that the Cullens are vampires. But they are bound by a treaty of non-disclosure in return for the Cullens never setting foot in La Push. He wonders if anyone would break the treaty to tell Bella about him.

Chapter 8: Ghost

Edward neglects the visiting vampires to keep an eye on Bella. He can't be at school for a few days because it is sunny, but he can still watch from the shadows. He is very amused when Mike tries to get a date with her, but Bella turns him down. Edward is impressed that she doesn't just turn him down, but turns his attentions towards Jessica, who really likes him.

Edward regularly watches Bella, trying to discern if and how much she likes him. The entire time he is conflicted. He wants Bella to be in love with him, but at the same time, he knows this is dangerous for her. So he wishes that she reject him, but dreads it at the same time. He continues doing his sweeps, and surveillance, to protect her.

He plans to follow her to Port Angeles, where she plans to do some shopping with Jessica and Angela. He does meet the vampire guests before they leave, but he's aloof and thinking of Bella.

Chapter 9: Port Angeles

Because it is so sunny, Edward drives into Port Angeles in a car with tinted windows. He can't follow Bella freely, but rather stay in the shadows while it is still daytime. He tries to watch her through other peoples' thoughts, Jessica's, primarily because they are so loud.

He is amused at Jessica's ruminations regarding herself, Bella, and Tyler. But he is lost in thought and only realizes at a latency that Bella isn't with the other two girls because she went off shopping on her own. Jessica isn't too concerned, though Angela is worried about what Bella might think if they stay apart too long.

Edward is overcome with worry and desperately scans other peoples' minds hoping to find her. He also braves walking out of the car while the sun is still up. He keeps to the shadows, but it is still a big risk.

He follows Bella's scent as much as he can and resorts to the car again when he loses track of it. He scans through peoples' minds as he drives, and finally, he finds her. The mind focused on her is that of a dangerous criminal.

A criminal, with a few drunk buddies, who is intent on assaulting and killing Bella. He has her cornered, but she isn't showing fear as she braces. Edward drives, anxious to get a sign for where exactly they are. He finally sees it in the mind of one of the criminal's friends, and he floors the gas pedal.

He drives the car right between the criminals and Bella, and she rushes to get in the car. Though Edward is hard-pressed to go after the criminal and kill him, he puts Bella's safety first and drives away.

Such is his rage at the criminals, and especially the leader, that he is overcome with murderous intent. He has to ask Bella to distract him so that he can cool down some. Bella does help him, talking about how she despises how Tyler is telling everyone that he's taking Bella to the prom.

When Bella asks him what is wrong, he confesses that he has to keep himself from going after the men that tried to assault her. He expects Bella to be appalled or frightened, but she isn't. When he realizes she hasn't eaten all day, he takes her to dinner. The other two girls have already eaten, so they leave them alone.

During dinner, Edward completely ignores the charmed waitress's advances. Instead, he comes clean to Bella, telling her that he followed her to Port Angeles to protect her. Edward doesn't pretend to be normal anymore. He tells her how he can read people's minds and narrates exactly how he struggled to find her in time.

Bella listens carefully, asking him questions about how the mind-reading works. She also says she has another theory about what he is, but will talk about it only when they return to Edward's car.

Chapter 10: Theory

Once in the car, Edward speeds too much and frightens Bella. He slows down and demands to hear her theory.

Bella explains that when she went to the beach, Billy Black's son Jacob was there. He talked to her about Quileute legends that his father believed. Jacob himself doesn't believe the myths, but he told Bella anyway because they involved the Cullens. Jacob told Bella that the Cullens were vampires.

This is how Bella pieced together the mystery around Edward and surmised that he must be a vampire in reality.

Edward is stunned when Bella tells him that even if he is a vampire, it doesn't matter to her. He can't wrap his mind around her disregard for the apparent danger.

All the secrets revealed between them, Edward answers her questions about vampirism and how many assumptions are myths. He tells her that it's not a myth that vampires drink blood, even though the Cullens abstain.

He even confesses how it is hard for him to keep from biting Bella. Bella admits that she needs to be near Edward, even though he's a vampire. That it hurts her to be away from him as much as it hurts him.

Edward drops her off at her father's house and drives off, elated that Bella loves him back. He decides to keep from killing the criminals that assaulted her because he doesn't want Bella to love a murderer. Still, he doesn't want to allow such criminals on the streets, so he goes to Carlisle with the problem.

Carlisle is very proud of him and reassures him that he will deal with it. They drive off together, and Edward shows Carlile where to find the criminal. He leaves to keep from attacking the man himself, trusting Carlisle to take care of it.

Edward goes to Bella's bedroom to watch her sleep, and he becomes happy hearing her say his name.

Chapter 11: Interrogations

Edward picks up Bella in the morning, to drive her to school. He is delighted to have her sit by him, to have his love be requited.

When they arrive at the school, Jessica is bowled over to see them together. The school, in general, pays attention to them as a couple. Edward tells Bella it would give him pleasure if she confirms Jessica's theory that they have been secretly dating. He spends the rest of the school day hungrily listening to the conversations Bella has with Jessica about him.

His family, Rosalie especially, is shocked to realize that Bella knows about their nature, as Edward has lunch with Bella at the school cafeteria. Edward knows he'll have to deal with them after school.

They declare their deep caring for each other again, and Edward admits he feels that if he loves her enough, he should leave her. Bella will not hear of it. Changing the subject, they talk about the drive to Seattle. Bella is open to doing other things than going to Seattle at Edward's suggestion.

He tells her that it will be sunny, and so he has to stay away from people. He tells her he'll show her how he looks like in the sun if she comes with him. Bella agrees. When she asks him about his hunting and what animal he prefers to have, he feels how his siblings are angered to hear him tell Bella everything.

Chapter 12: Complications

Edward is longing for Bella physically as well as emotionally, but he tells himself that such a thing is off-limits. It would be too dangerous for her. Still, when he meets up with Emmett, Emmett points out that he looks happy. Edward doesn't deny it.

He asks Emmett to help him do a charade for the benefit of Angela Weber. Edward is fond of the girl because her thoughts are always so benign and caring for everyone, including Bella. He knows from reading her thoughts that she wants a boy, Ben, to ask her to the prom. And he also knows that Ben is interested in Angela but has little courage to walk up to her to ask her.

Edward and Emmett pretend to talk about how he intended to ask Angela to the prom but wouldn't because he heard she was interested in Ben. Ben is surprised and delighted, and he is determined to ask Angela now. Edward is also happy he could do something for the girl.

Edward is pleased as he hears Mike's thoughts and disappointment at confirming that Bella is in love with Edward. They are having the conversation during Gym. When the teacher forces Bella to play, she has an accident that hurts both her and Mike. She's allowed not to play afterward. Edward is waiting for her after Gym ends, highly amused.

He takes her home after school and explains to her why it would be dangerous for her to be present while he hunts. He still has a strong urge to be away from her, for her protection, together with his intense attraction.

Returning home, Edward is confronted by Rosalie about telling Bella everything about them. Edward tells her that Bella already knew from the stories Jacob Black told her. That stalls Rosalie's tirade. Carlisle settles things by reassuring Jasper about Alice's safety. Edward realizes he understands Jasper and his reactions a lot more now that he's in love with Bella. Rosalie, too, points out that he has changed in his reactions, and about how he finds things he cared about before insignificant, like his car.

Chapter 13: Another Complication

As he takes her to school the next morning, Edward asks Bella all kinds of questions about her tastes and preferences. He wants to know what will please her in terms of gifts, as well as get to know her even more.

Later in class, he's incensed to realize that there is a bet going on between his siblings on whether Bella will live or die on the weekend, he plans to spend with her. Emmett apologizes, and Edward concedes because he knows it's hard for the other vampires to understand his position.

Bella talks to him about Phoenix and how she likes the scorching sun and the light. He hears the fondness in her voice about the city, and then he asks her about her own house and room. The descriptions she gives are indicative of her relationship with her mother. Her mother might love her, but she doesn't play the role of a mother for Bella.

Upon return to Bella's home, Edward is dismayed to see that Billy Black and his son Jacob are visiting. Another complication that arises is that they see him with Bella. Edward hears Billy's thoughts and how he's aware of what Edward is.

Despite that, Billy doesn't tell Charlie anything and leaves soon enough. He knows that Billy will be talking about the encounter with the elders in La Push. He tells Carlisle, who is certain the treaty won't be breached. He urges Edward to spend time with Esme, his mother.

Edward goes, and Esme treats him soothingly as they play the piano together. She reassures him that he will not hurt Bella and encourages him since she makes him happy.

Are you enjoying the book so far?

If so, please help us reach more readers by taking 30 seconds to write just a few words on Amazon.

Or, you can choose to leave one later...

Chapter 14: Closer

It's still Edward's turn to ask questions, and he asks Bella about dating. It turns out she hasn't really had any dates nor any boy she was interested in. Edward tells her it has been the same for him.

Alice finally meets Bella. Because Edward has to leave with Alice, he gets Bella's permission to fetch her truck so that she can drive home on her own. Bella grants it, and they go to Bella's empty house to retrieve the truck key and park it at the school for her. The sheer intimacy of this implies how close Bella and the Cullens are becoming.

Chapter 15: Probability

Alice warns Edward that the vision where he drinks Bella's blood, killing her, has returned. She tells him that the location in the vision is the meadow, where he plans to take Bella the next day.

Edward tries to find a way to avoid this by not going to the meadow and leaving. But the vision never changes. Alice also shows him that if he does leave, Bella will sink into a debilitating depression. When Edward desperately presses Alice to show him a better path for the future, she shows him the option of Bella becoming a vampire. She adds that there are other futures, but all pass through the meadow. If she survives the meadow, if he manages not to kill her, then there will be time for different futures going forward.

Finally, Alice shows him the future where Bella lives on with him, but as a mortal. Everything hinges, however, on Edward finding a way to avoid killing her at the meadow.

Edward goes through an intense emotional struggle, but he decides to be the Edward that Bella wants and needs. Alice tells him that this is strengthening the probabilities in favor of Bella surviving.

Determined, Edward prepares for the outing to the meadow, dressing so he'll be able to show himself to Bella under the sun.

On the eve of the excursion, he remembers his first years as a vampire. He'd started off abstaining from human blood since Carlisle was the one that created him, and he practiced abstinence as well. But when they met with other vampires that hunted normally, Edward decided to leave Carlisle and try it on his own, because they referred to drinking human blood as the greatest joy in life.

Edward hunted humans for years, always keeping to hunting criminals such as murderers and rapists, but never felt this ecstasy. He always missed Carlisle and Esme, and eventually, he returned to them and stopped hunting humans.

He considers now that the greatest joy in life for him is Bella. Alice calls him to tell him the odds that Bella survives are even stronger.

Chapter 16: The Knot

On the drive to the meadow, Bella tells Edward that she has made sure that people don't know she is with him. She directly tells him it's to protect him should anything happen, which distresses Edward.

They hike to the meadow, and Edward asks her assorted questions about herself, trying to brace himself for what is coming. Bella's complete trust in him makes him anxious but also determined to deserve it.

Once they reach the meadow, he steps into the sun in front of her.

Chapter 17: Confessions

Seeing Edward in the sun makes a profound impression on Bella. At first, she is terrified that he is burning because he is shining so brightly. But he stops her from rushing to him, needing her to keep her distance.

She approaches him slowly, cautiously, as he carefully concentrates on keeping his vampire instincts from flaring. Bella calls him beautiful, which surprises him. He expected her to find him monstrous.

But when Bella comes too close, Edward's instincts kick in. He raises his hand to make her keep her distance, and he works hard to occupy his mind so that his instincts remain under control. When he seems to have managed, Bella approaches him and strokes him tentatively. Edward likes it immensely and lets her know.

They come closer and closer, but then, just as they are about to kiss, he almost bites her. He rushes away from her in a fit of fear and anger. He rants about how easy it is to kill her as he throws a tantrum, destroying some of the flora in the beautiful meadow.

Soon though, seeing Bella's terror, he comes to his senses and reassures her that he won't hurt her. Slowly, painfully, he explains to her for the first time the true irresistibility of her blood and the effect it has on him. He explains his early behavior, before and after the accident, and how he struggled with all his anguish and effort in keeping her safe. Safe from himself.

Bella finally understands his erratic behavior of before, as well as the high risk she's running being close to Edward: Edward tells her how Emmett killed the humans whose blood had the same effect on him.

And yet, she decides to stay with him because being away from him is worse than death to her.

Overcome with love for her, Edward listens to her heart and feels her pulse in a close embrace. He then realizes that he has no desire to drain her of blood, despite the sheer allure it still has for him. He realizes how his struggle was in his mind, mostly acting as a self-fulfilling prophecy than anything else.

The realization is hugely liberating for Edward, and he is light with happiness. He manages to embrace and kiss Bella at the top of her head before agreeing that they must return. He is now positive that he will never run the risk of killing her, ever again.

He takes Bella on his back to show her how he travels through the forest, but his super-speed terrifies Bella a lot more than the threat of biting her did. He helps her work through her dizziness and shock. And as he's fondly teasing her and helping her, their first real kiss comes seamlessly.

Chapter 18: Mind Over Matter

On the way back, Edward tells Bella his real age upon her request. He then narrates how Carlisle changed him when he was dying of the Spanish Flu. He tells her how Carlisle found Esme, then Rosalie. He tells her how Rosalie took a dying Emmett to Carlisle, begging him to turn him because she was unsure she could do it herself. He also tells her how Alice and Jasper found Carlisle and already had their conscience formed. Edward describes how Alice sees visions.

He takes Bella home and comes in with her. He watches her prepare food. Edward keeps nothing from Bella, including how he has been sneaking into her bedroom to watch her sleep. Bella isn't turned off; instead, she's worried only about what she said while sleeping.

When Charlie comes, Edward hides in her bedroom. Bella doesn't want Edward to go. She goes through the motions of talking with her father, but she quickly retires so she can be with Edward. They share moments of great affection, and Edward isn't in the least tempted to bite her. His countenance is light and gentle, and Bella is amazed. He explains to her that once he made his decision to conquer his nature, he has mind over matter.

They talk fondly to each other and eventually snuggle in Bella's bed. They talk even of marriage, and how neither of them has had sex before. Bella finally sleeps, feeling safe in Edward's arms. In her sleep, she says, "Edward, I love you."

Chapter 19: Home

With Bella sleeping deeply, Edward hurries to his house to prepare. He will bring Bella to meet his family, and he must talk to Rosalie, who is the only one hostile and jealous of Bella.

Rosalie is defensive when Edward goes to talk to her, but she explains that her deep animosity towards Bella stems from the fact that she will throw her life away. A life that Rosalie covets, because Rosalie longs to be human again.

Edward is shaken by her words and assures Rosalie that he won't let Bella become a vampire. Rosalie is doubtful. She does entertain the idea of tolerating Bella. However, when she realizes that he intends to bring her on the same day, she decides to leave for the day.

Edward returns to Bella's home and invites her to meet his family. Bella is worried they may disapprove, but he reassures her. When Edward suggests that she introduce him to Charlie as her boyfriend, Bella is irritated because she wants a more serious relationship than that. Edward reassures her that he will stay with her until she tires of him, anyway.

Bella gets ready to meet the Cullens, They kiss, and Bella nearly faints because she's so enthralled. After a bit of teasing, they drive out to the Cullen house.

Carlisle and Esme are thrilled to meet her. Alice, too, is excited to be able to talk to her more. Jasper is on his best behavior. Emmett is not there, because he's with Rosalie, helping her calm down.

After a few pleasantries, the Cullens leave Edward and Bella alone. Edward plays the piano for her, including the song she inspired. Bella is very self-conscious. Then Edward talks to her about Rosalie and how she envies Bella.

Edward then shows Bella around the house, and she sees a very old wooden cross on the wall. Edward tells her it is from Carlisle's time in the 1600s. He then tells her of Carlisle's origins.

Chapter 20: Carlisle

Edward leads Bella in Carlisle's study to continue his story. Carlisle looks happy to have them but tells Edward to keep narrating his story since he has to leave to go to the hospital. Edward shows Bella a wall full of framed works, which he uses to carry the story along for her.

He tells her how, when Carlisle realized he had become a vampire, he tried to kill himself. When this proved unsuccessful, despite the various ways he tried to accomplish it, Carlisle stayed away from humans as much as possible. He then swam to France and eventually ended up in Italy, where he met other vampires, including the Volturi. When his determination to abstain from human blood became a source of constant friction, Carlisle decided to migrate to the New World, where he remained.

Bella asks Edward whether he remained with Carlisle ever since he was created, and Edward confesses that he didn't, telling her of his days of human hunting. His mind strays to the last man he killed, a man that would have hurt a child, but Edward stopped him just before he managed. He recalls how the man was relieved he was stopped, but it made Edward also stop his hunting.

Edward generally expresses to her how he expects that there probably will be a point where some information he tells Bella will turn her away from him. Bella reassures him that this won't occur.

Edward then shows Bella his room. He is happy that Bella knows everything about him now, and becomes playful. Then, Alice and Jasper come to invite them to a vampire baseball game. Bella, of course, accepts.

Chapter 21: The Game

Edward returns Bella to her home so she can eat and rest until the game. Upon return, however, they realize that Billy Black and Jacob have arrived. He intends to warn Charlie about Edward.

Edward is angry, but Bella tells him she will handle this. Edward agrees and leaves but not before goading Billy by kissing Bella's throat. Bella tells Billy not to interfere in her affairs and that she is fully aware of Edward's nature. This surprises Billy, but he does agree to back off and not warn Charlie about Edward.

Edward follows the Blacks to La Push. Through Jacob's thoughts, he remembers how Billy had reacted when Carlisle called to alert the man that the Cullens were returning. He had been agitated but remembered the treaty. Edward also remembers how Charlie hadn't considered Billy's warnings regarding Carlisle when Carlisle started working at the hospital.

Returning home, he reports the situation to Carlisle, and then he tries to coax Rosalie into participating in the game. She reluctantly agrees, which pleases Emmett. Edward has him decide not to do anything that would scare Bella.

He returns to Bella's house, where Bella introduces him to Charlie as her boyfriend. Charlie and Edward interact politely for a while, and then Edward leaves with Bella. After driving for some time, and playfully convincing her to let him carry her while he runs at super speed, he takes her to an off-road area. The Cullens refer to it simply as the clearing because it is empty of trees.

The Cullens are all there, including Rosalie. Esme sits with Bella as they prepare the game and set out the rules. Then they begin playing. Bella is amazed and enthused, watching them play with their super strength and super speed. As they engage more in the game, even shouting cuss words at each other as the score fluctuates, Bella is thoroughly entertained.

But, the game is cut short because Alice sees three stranger vampires are about to arrive at the clearing. They heard the game and are simply looking to participate. However, this is very dangerous because Bella is there.

They decide not to rush Bella away because she's safer while surrounded by seven protector vampires. Still, there is a big risk approaching, and Edward feels guilty for not having foreseen it. All they can do, as they continue the game and hope the other vampires won't cause trouble, is wait for them to arrive.

Chapter 22: The Hunt

Edward can read the thoughts of the three vampires that arrive, named Laurent, James, and Victoria. They are apprehensive, but since they are friendly, they believe they can be on good terms with the seven vampires that are watching them approach.

Edward is amazed that Jasper is using his powers in a way he hadn't before seen, which is to camouflage Bella and himself by inspiring the newcomers' gaze to turn away from them. Carlisle, as well, is using his high skill in affable diplomacy. Things seem to be going well, and Carlisle almost succeeds in taking the three vampires away from the clearing.

However, at the last moment, the breeze brings Bella's smell right in the path of the vampires. Their countenances immediately change, and James just lunges for her. Edward blocks him, which surprises James, and makes him even more determined to get to Bella.

While Laurent relents and assures the Cullens that they won't be hunting Bella, Edward knows that this is only temporary. James is now thrilled with the challenge of the hunt, and he will come back for her.

As they leave, James' eyes fall on Alice, and he seems to be surprised to see her there. He follows Laurent and Carlisle, but Edward knows he'll break away to come back for Bella as soon as he can.

Edward panics and tries to rush to take Bella far away. But Bella opposes him because Charlie will think he kidnapped her, which will get the FBI on the Cullens and ruin their life in general, not just in Forks. Edward can't control his emotions, because he has realized that James is a tracker: a vampire skilled in tracking and finding his targets, who doesn't stop unless he has succeeded.

Finally, however, Alice and Bella manage to get him to pause and listen so they can make a viable plan that will protect both Bella and the Cullens. They decide to let Bella go home and tell Charlie she's leaving for Phoenix. Then, she will rejoin the Cullens, who will split into three groups. One to protect Charlie in case James targets him, one to be a ruse for James to follow, and one with Bella.

The group with Bella will go to Phoenix after they convince James that she is only pretending to go there. The group that is the ruse will lure James away with Bella's smell and possibly trap him to deal with him. The plan requires that Bella and Edward split so that Edward can be the ruse James follows.

Chapter 23: Goodbyes

Bella returns home and pretends to have broken up with Edward. She throws a tantrum in front of Charlie and declares that she's returning to her mother. Charlie tries to coax her to stay for a few days, but she says some hurtful words, and he lets her go. Bella feels terrible about it, but consoles herself that she will soon return to make amends.

They all go to the Cullen house, where Carlisle is with Laurent. Laurent is very apologetic and regretful that he ever was with James and Victoria. He warns them that James never gives up on his prey and that he is very intelligent. Edward sees that James has won against stronger vampires through his slyness and wit.

After Laurent leaves, Esme and Rosalie take Bella's truck. Edward pockets socks with Bella's smell. Carlisle and Emmett go with him. Alice and Jasper go with Bella after she has a heartfelt goodbye with Edward.

Edward hates being separated, but he is determined to make the plan work.

Chapter 24: Ambush

The teams communicate with satellite phones, mainly so that Alice's visions can guide Edward, Emmett, and Carlisle to lure away James successfully. It's a tantalizing game of cat and mouse, where every communication counts and every choice made can spell disaster.

Edward's team manages to lure James away successfully, but they stop and try to ambush him too soon. James manages to escape by diving into the water, in which he can't be tracked. He also has realized that this team does not have Bella.

Edward's team now is the one giving chase, trying to discern where James will go and apprehend him. James proves to be a very cunning adversary. He's always one step ahead in evading them until finally, he manages to lose them entirely in Vancouver, by flying away from a small private airstrip.

After letting the others know James escaped, Edward's team returns to Forks, only to receive an agonized phone call by Alice. She has seen that James is going to Phoenix to find Bella's mother, Renee.

Edward's team hurries to take a commercial flight to Phoenix to meet up with Alice, Jasper, and Bella so they can evacuate Bella and then protect her mother.

Chapter 25: Race

When Edward, Carlisle, and Emmett arrive at the airport, they meet up with Alice and Jasper, but Bella isn't there. She has left behind a note of apology and rushed to James to protect her mother. James has blackmailed her with Renee.

It becomes a race against time to catch up to Bella to save her from James. Alice struggles to understand where James is taking her. Edward steals a very fast car, and everyone takes off in it.

It is agony for Edward to drive while Alice has visions of Bella in the hands of James. Alice tries to focus on finding the way to where he's keeping her. They switch cars when the one they are in becomes flagged as stolen, and roadblocks are being set up. They also cause a highway accident to stall the police chasing them.

With the visions of Bella in James' hands, Edward is considering suicide on the eventuality of Bella's death. But they manage to reach the building where he's keeping her, and sneak up to the place.

Edward attacks.

Chapter 26: Blood

Edward crashes through the door, right at the moment when James is over Bella's bloodied and motionless body. He yanks him off her and throws him to Emmett and Jasper. Emmett and Jasper summarily kill James by tearing him apart.

Carlisle rushes to where Bella is lying in a pool of blood and begins giving her first aid, with Edward being troubled and full of anguish. Bella has consciousness, though, and it looks like she will be salvageable.

It is then that they realize that James bit her hand. The vampire's venom is in her veins, and Bella has already begun changing. All hope to save her seems lost, at least in her mortal state.

Edward can't tolerate it, and he begs for a different way. Carlisle suggests that he suck out the venom while there is still time to reverse the effect. Alice promises to warn him when to stop. Edward is horrified because it means that he will bite and drink Bella's blood, at least as long as there is venom in her.

Carlisle tells him that it's his decision, but he has to decide fast. Edward takes the chance and bites into her injured hand, sucking out her blood with the venom. The taste of her blood throws him into physical ecstasy and a hunger for more, to have it all until Bella is drained.

It's a terrible struggle for him to even have an awareness of what he's doing at all, let alone stop. Alice begs him to stop, seeing that he has gone past the point necessary, and he still doesn't. It's only when he hears Bella's voice begging him to stay with her that he finds the presence of mind and will to stop.

Bella is saved from being changed into a vampire, and they gently prepare to take her to a hospital. It turns out James tricked Bella. He didn't actually have Renee.

Chapter 27: Chores

Taking Bella to the hospital, and covering up the incident, is the next task at hand. Carlisle directs them to a hospital where he has a friend colleague, and he enjoys recognition and respect.

Since they are already in a stolen car, even taking Bella to the hospital is tricky. Alice goes through various scenarios of how to do it, as well as how to cover the incident up as an accident, always seeing into the future to check if it will work.

After too many times of rerunning the scenario, Alice finds the perfect solution, with all the tiny details necessary to make everything work smoothly. They park the car away from the hospital cameras and transport Bella in the ER.

Among the commotion, Alice slips by and steals blood bags of Bella's blood type. She then checks in to the hotel Bella was supposedly staying and stages a bloody accident scene, making it look like Bella tripped over a flight of stairs and smashed into a window. They have Rosalie send Bella's truck to Phoenix, to make it look like she drove to the city on her own, as she had told Charlie.

Chapter 28: Three Conversations

Once Bella is seen to, and on the mend, Carlisle calls Charlie. He lets him know Bella had an accident, but she will be fine. Charlie is very obliged, especially when Carlisle says he and Edward will stay with her since Charlie has to be at a trial. He is also concerned over Bella's strong emotions over Edward, but Carlisle reassures him about that too.

Next comes Bella's mother, Renee, to see her. She is distraught, and Edward realizes that her thoughts project to other people, compelling them to respond to her. Renee is impressed by Edward but worried he will break Bella's heart. He reassures her he will do nothing of the sort.

Alice comes later and brings Edward a camera. It is James' camera, which he had used to film everything he did to Bella. He intended to emotionally torture Edward and get him to come after James. In the video, he watches how Bella is bravely talking to James until he gloats about how he managed to snatch her before it occurred to Edward to change Bella into a vampire. He narrates how, in the past, he had hunted another mortal female, Alice. And he didn't manage to get her because another vampire changed her, thus eliminating her from James' targets.

Then he tries to get Bella to call for Edward, so that her final moments pleading for him will be recorded in the camera. But still, Bella refuses, trying to tell Edward not to go after James. James is enraged and throws her around in the room until Edward sees himself burst in to save Bella. He sees some of what happened afterward until Alice noticed the camera and switched it off.

Edward is overcome with emotion, and he finds himself praying to "Bella's God" since he feels he is damned, or disconnected from any deity or divinity. He prays for wellbeing nonetheless, for help to protect Bella from himself.

Chapter 29: Inevitability

When Bella wakes up, Edward is there for her to see. They speak fondly to each other, and Bella is merely happy that things have been taken care of. She only truly becomes distressed when Edward makes a hint of needing to go. He refrains from doing that again and reassures her that he will be there, even during her mom's visit.

Renee is glad to see Bella awake. But the more she is reassured that her daughter is fine, the more she slips back to a more self-centered way of thinking. Still, she offers to take Bella with her to stay with Phil, her second husband. Bella refuses this and urges Renee to take a phone call she's expecting from Phil.

Bella and Edward then discuss why he didn't let her turn into a vampire. Bella seems eager to become a vampire to be with Edward forever. Edward reminds her that she still has connections to her parents, who she'd need to leave. This stalls Bella for a while, but the idea stays with her. She doesn't want to live and die a mortal.

Epilogue: An Occasion

Renee left soon, convinced by Bella that everything was ok and she should return to Florida. Edward and Carlisle take care of Bella, and they return her home to Forks when she's ready to be discharged.

Edward can tell that Charlie blames Edward for Bella's predicament, and he doesn't blame him. In fact, Edward agrees with him, feeling the guilt of having exposed Bella to the danger of other vampires. However, Alice keeps taking care of Bella at her home, and Charlie likes her a lot. He also feels obliged to Carlisle for all his help.

When they return to school, their classmates believe the story about Bella's accident. As for why she was in Phoenix, the explanation is provided by Jessica's theorizing. It is, of course, wrong, but it establishes Edward and Bella as a couple.

Edward still plans to leave as soon as Bella is ready. But while he's around, he enjoys being with her. When the time for the prom comes, Bella is mostly healed. Edward and Alice invite Bella for an occasion but don't tell her she will be going to the prom with him.

Alice gives Bella a makeover, and Edward dresses very formally. Edward wants to give the fun memories that she can have when she grows up and marries some other, mortal man, which she will tell her children.

When Bella realizes they are going to the prom, she is distressed because she fears she will be clumsy and break her other leg as well. She's still wearing a cast on one from the incident. Edward reassures her that he won't let her be harmed in any way. He has her step on his feet so he can dance with her. Bella enjoys herself despite her initial horror.

Jacob arrives, feeling very uncomfortable, to relay a message to Bella from his father, Billy. The message is that they will be watching and that they're convinced Edward was to blame for her predicament. Bella takes this well, and she treats Jacob kindly, which makes Jacob's crush on her stronger.

Later, Edward asks her what she thought she was being dressed up for, if she truly was surprised that he took her to the prom. Bella is reluctant to confess, but in the end, she says that she is expected to be turned into a vampire. Edward repeats that he will never do this to her, despite her willingness. He teases her a little about it, but he still promises that he will never leave her- unless he absolutely has to.

Analysis of Key Characters

Edward Cullen

Told from Edward's point of view, we could say that this love affair that he has with Bella is his personal journey and challenge.

At the story beginning, Edward is stagnant: he believes there is nothing for him to experience in the world. He also has low self-esteem, thinking himself a monster. At the same time, he ironically thinks he is as perfect as his nature allows: he has great self-control and is looked up to by his siblings as a great example to follow.

When Bella comes into his life, she upturns all of these assumptions in one fell swoop. His self-control completely collapses when he is around her. His ability to read minds doesn't work on her. All of the things in which he prided himself for excellence now fail him. At the same time, she intrigues him. He can't understand the workings of her mind. As a result, she steadily inspires a mental and emotional allure that enhances, as well as counterbalances, the physical one of the predator.

The duality of Edward's character seems to seep into the realm of psychology more than physical biology. His challenge is to realize that. Edward doesn't seem to understand at first that he has already been controlling his vampiric impulses for human blood for several decades, something that is unthinkable to other vampires. That means that he already has physical control over his natural urges.

When Bella comes along, he attributes his complete transformation into a predator to her delicious blood fragrance. But even at this first encounter, he manages to reel himself in. Bella serves as the stimulus that forces Edward to come to terms with his own nature in a way that he can enjoy life and accept happiness for himself.

When he manages to open himself to being loved, his urges considerably recede. The final trial at the meadow hinges a lot more on acceptance of himself as a complete entity rather than resistance to the part of himself he finds abhorrent. Once he manages to accept himself enough not to fear himself, he can control all of his nature and thus stops being a threat to Bella.

Bella Swan

Bella is the embodiment of pure love. All of her motivations stem from selfless love: she comes to Forks to make her mother's life easier. She takes care of her father in a reversal of roles. She looks after her classmates at school by indirectly, but definitely, taking steps to give them happiness or protect them from distress. Bella's own wishes always take second priority when they clash with those of others.

When she meets Edward, she falls instantly in love with him. Even when she thinks this love is unrequited, she acts in ways that accommodate what she perceives to be his wishes. When Edward shows her that he loves her back, she gives herself completely to this love. As with everyone, Edward becomes her priority: his safety and that of his family's come first and her own life second.

Bella's love for Edward is pure and absolute, and in it, she becomes trusting and fearless. It unnerves Edward, but it also challenges him to rise to that love and become worthy of it. Bella is the stimulus that makes Edward strive to push his own limits and become a better person.

Carlisle Cullen

Carlisle is Edward's father in every way that is significant to Edward. He is the vampire that made him, and he is the man that gave him guidance and shelter twice without judging Edward for his mistakes.

Carlisle believes in Edward a lot more than Edward does in his own self. He also is a character that loves fiercely and purely, but in a different way than Bella: his concern manifests in a very moral level, with clear, hard choices that are tantamount to ideology.

Although his nature as a vampire is to be a predator to humans, he has become a doctor, a healer for them. Although vampires are mostly nomadic, he chooses to put down roots as much as his need to keep his nature secret allows. Although vampires don't have families, Carlisle has created one.

Carlisle represents the triumph of humanity over base instinct and illustrates that this triumph can only stem from love.

Alice Cullen

Alice is a vampire with the unique ability to see the future. Edward, but also all the other Cullens, look to her to tell them how to act to get a positive outcome in things they need or want to achieve.

Alice represents fate. How much of peoples' future is set in stone? Alice is a character that explores that. How much can you change the future if you have a warning about what's coming?

There are some things that Edward can change or avert, and yet there are others he can't avoid, no matter how much he changes the choices he makes. It seems that fate is flexible but not completely malleable.

Alice is also fallible. There are estimates about the future that she has made, which end up being wrong. This happens for many reasons, but mostly because characters subtly change their determination or their motivations. The future is a very fragile thing: our slightest choice, action, or inaction can drastically change it.

Major Symbols

Shadows

Shadows play a significant role in *Midnight Sun*: Forks is very dim, and the vampires can only be at ease within shadows during the day in a constant hide and seek.

But the vampires can't be harmed from the sun. If they step into the sun, they won't be burned or killed. They hide from it solely to protect themselves from human perception, reaction, and persecution. It can be argued that society is the only reason they need shadows to hide and protect them, be it the human or the vampire one since the Volturi demand secrecy.

But within the story, Edward only finds happiness when he steps into the sun and lets Bella see him fully. He only feels light and at ease when he hides nothing from Bella, the same way he hides nothing from his family.

Shadows are at times protection, but they mostly present hindrance. Bella is almost assaulted in Port Angeles because Edward can't go out in the sun and has to limit himself in whatever shadows are cast by the buildings. He can't be with her in public on sunny days to avoid being seen with his sparkling diamond skin.

Shadows hide otherness, but the need for shadows causes burden and anguish to those who are forced to stay within them.

Blood

Blood is a symbol of desire in *Midnight Sun*. It can be construed to be the symbol of base desire or lust. When Edward first sees Bella, her blood smells so sweet to him that he almost loses himself and his control. This makes him feel hate for her, aversion, and cause him to treat her erratically and with hostility.

When he falls in love with Bella, though her blood still mesmerizes him, it doesn't cause him to be overwhelmed with the urge to bite into her. When he entirely devotes himself to her and this love, the urge recedes fully despite the allure remaining.

Carlisle, who is portrayed as having completely vanquished his vices, never is tempted by human blood of any kind.

Motifs

Hades and Persephone

The ancient Greek myth of Hades and Persephone, the king and queen of the underworld, is a frequent motif and analogy. Edward is Hades, king of the dead. He is one of the best vampires, excellent in everything and with the added gift of reading minds. Bella is Persephone, his queen, whom he abducts from her world and brings into his. She becomes mesmerized and can't leave. He likens every bit of information, everything that she likes about him and his world to pomegranate seeds: the food Persephone ate and which kept her forever in the underworld. And he makes that analogy because it's the allure of all these things that he tells her that keep Bella charmed by the concept of being a vampire. In a very real way, she is bound to the vampire world by her enthusiasm for it as well as by her love of Edward.

It is not by chance that the final commitment, the one that marks Edward and Bella as a definite couple, takes place in a meadow in bloom: Persephone was taken to the underworld through precisely such a meadow.

This motif is so dominant throughout the story that it even informs the cover of the book: hands offering a pomegranate with blood-red seeds against a black background.

The Pantheon of the Vampires

Although we are told that it's unusual for vampires to have extra gifts or powers, the Cullens seem to all have them: Edward can read minds, Alice can see the future, Emmett is extraordinarily strong, Jasper can affect emotions, Rosalie is stunningly beautiful, and Carlisle has extraordinary charm and compassion. Esme doesn't seem to have an extra gift, but she doesn't need to: she is the wife of the patriarch, just like Hera is the wife of Zeus.

In *Midnight Sun*, the vampires are godlike, but in the sense of the ancient pantheons rather than our current concept of abstract divinity. They have drawbacks and virtues, while their acts, beliefs, and vices affect the lives of mortals. There is even a painting on Carlisle's wall that illustrates vampires as gods.

Themes

Mind Over Matter

The soul is willing, but the flesh is too weak: that's where the mind comes in. *Midnight Sun* is about internal struggle. Edward fights with his own nature for dominion over himself. The aspects of vampirism that render him a monster, the need to hunt for humans without concern for them, is the begin-all and end-all for him.

Despite his love for Bella, he continually struggles with the natural urge to treat her as prey, not as an individual. It is only when he manages to rely on his mind fully, and force of will, that he conquers the natural impulse and urge that has turned every vampire into a wild predator.

Love Is Eternal Life

Edward starts off believing that being a vampire makes him deprived of actual life and living. He feels that he's floating in a purgatory of sorts, devoid of emotions and challenges that make a mortal feel alive. What yanks him from this limbo is the love he develops for Bella. By loving her, he begins to be ravaged by intense emotions: devotion, jealousy, concern, worry, elation, and happiness. Through love, he is able to truly live again.

The same goes for Carlisle, who loves Esme, but also humanity. He leads a life, rather than a half-dead existence, because his love allows him to feel compelling emotions for other people. It also makes him be a father and a protector as he creates a cohesive, loving family.

Vampires like James that don't harbor love become monsters that lose their individuality and personality. Once they succumb to an existence without love, they are nothing more than animals or predators that cannot emotionally connect to others. They become interchangeable threats rather than unique individuals.

Discussion Questions

1. Why has Bella come to Forks?

2. What doesn't Bella like about Forks?

3. Why have the Cullens chosen to live in Forks?

4. In what major ways are the Cullens different than other vampires?

5. Why is high school like purgatory for Edward?

6. What does Edward initially think about Bella?

7. What is the first thing that makes Edward think about Bella as better than the rest?

8. How old is Edward?

9. What does Edward think of Carlisle?

10. What does Edward think of Rosalie?

11. Except Bella, who does Edward think fondly of among the students, and why?

12. Who are Bella's friends in high school?

13. Who are the Blacks, and why are they significant for the Cullens?

14. Why does Rosalie hate the fact that Edward saved Bella from a car accident?

15. Why does Edward treat Bella coldly when, in reality, he really likes her?

16. How do Alice's visions of the future work?

17. Why does Edward begin talking to Bella and treat her well again?

18. What happens in the meadow?

19. Why is James hunting Bella?

20. How did Edward save Bella from becoming a vampire?

Thought-Provoking Discussion Questions

1. Why does Edward think of himself as a monster?

2. Why does Edward not think of Carlisle in this way?

3. Why doesn't Edward want Bella to become a vampire?

4. In what way do you think that Edward falls in love with Bella?

5. Why did Edward stop hunting for criminals? Why wasn't getting them off the streets enough?

6. What do you think made Carlisle be at peace with his nature? Why?

7. Why do most of the Cullens crave becoming human again?

8. What makes a vampire a monster?

9. Are vampires above human law?

10. Why is Edward able to stop drinking Bella's blood in the end?

11. Based on Alice's efforts to help Edward's predicaments, do you think fate is inescapable? Why/ why not?

12. Is Rosalie's animosity and hostility towards Bella shallow? Why/why not?

13. What makes a human a monster?

14. Is all life precious, as Carlisle believes, or are some lives more precious than others? In the end, does even Carlisle demonstrate some prioritizing about whose life is worth saving?

15. How would you characterize Edward's and Bella's love? What elements do you base your answer on?

Thank you for finishing the book!

Looks like you've enjoyed it! ☺

Please help us reach more readers by taking 30 seconds to write just a few words on Amazon now.

Warmest regards,

Omni Reads Team

CPSIA information can be obtained
at www.ICGtesting.com
Printed in the USA
LVHW081239250820
664180LV00019B/2291